C.1

Berenstain, Stan,
1923-

The Berenstain Bears
and the wheelchair
commando.

Too-Tall didn't really expect Harry to play. But he sure was having a ball teasing him.

"What do you say, Wheels?" he said. "I'll bet your fans would like to see what you can do on the basketball court."

The other cubs began to take Harry's side. "Cool it," someone said. "Yeah, cut it out," said another.

But to everyone's surprise, Harry wheeled himself right up to Too-Tall at center court and said, "Okay, I'll play."

BIG CHAPTER BOOKS

The Berenstain Bears and the Drug Free Zone

The Berenstain Bears and the New Girl in Town

The Berenstain Bears Gotta Dance!

The Berenstain Bears and the Nerdy Nephew

The Berenstain Bears Accept No Substitutes

The Berenstain Bears and the Female Fullback

The Berenstain Bears and the Red-Handed Thief

The Berenstain Bears
    and the Wheelchair Commando

Coming soon

The Berenstain Bears and the School Scandal Sheet

The Berenstain Bears at Camp Crush

The Berenstain Bears and the Galloping Ghost

The Berenstain Bears
and the WHEELCHAIR COMMANDO

by Stan & Jan Berenstain

A BIG CHAPTER BOOK™

Random House New York

Copyright © 1993 by Berenstain Enterprises, Inc.
All rights reserved under International and Pan-American Copyright
Conventions. Published in the United States by Random House, Inc.,
New York, and simultaneously in Canada by Random House of
Canada Limited, Toronto.

Library of Congress Cataloging-in-Publication Data
Berenstain, Stan.
The Berenstain Bears and the wheelchair commando /
by Stan and Jan Berenstain.
   p.   cm. — (A Big chapter book)
SUMMARY: Harry, a new student at Bear Country School who is
disabled and uses a wheelchair, has trouble making friends until the
others discover that he is really very much like them.
ISBN 0-679-84034-6 (pbk.) — ISBN 0-679-94034-0 (lib. bdg.)
[1. Physically handicapped—Fiction.   2. Wheelchairs—Fiction.
3. Schools—Fiction.   4. Bears—Fiction.]   I. Berenstain, Jan.
II. Title.   III. Series: Berenstain, Stan.   Big chapter book.
PZ7.B4483Bele   1993
[E]—dc20   93-8871

Manufactured in the United States of America   10 9 8 7 6 5 4 3 2 1

BIG CHAPTER BOOKS is a trademark of Berenstain Enterprises, Inc.

C·l

Contents

Chapter 1
The New Cub

Until Harry McGill moved into the house on Boxwood Drive, his neighbors-to-be didn't know much more about him than his name.

They knew he was a boy, and they knew he was about Brother Bear's age. But that was all. They had found that much out from

Millie McGrizz, Miz McGrizz's grown daughter. Millie was in the real-estate business. She had sold the house on Boxwood Drive to the McGills.

"Why does this new cub have to be a boy?" said Sister Bear as she walked home from school with Brother and Cousin Freddy. "I've got boys coming out of my ears!"

IV'E GOT BOYS COMING OUT OF MY EARS!

Brother groaned and Freddy laughed. Brother groaned because Sister was always saying things to get him going. Cousin Freddy laughed because he didn't have to live with Sister.

Brother thought for a moment, then smiled. "You're just saying that because we've got you outnumbered," he said.

It was true, in a way. Brother, Sister, and Cousin Freddy weren't together all the time, but they were together a lot. They walked to and from school together. Their families went places together. Their mothers were not only sisters but best friends. And although Sister was younger than Brother and Freddy, and in a lower grade, she usually touched base with them at lunch and recess. Even their other close friends thought of Brother, Sister, and Cousin Freddy as a trio.

"The truth is," said Brother, "more girls than boys have moved into the neighborhood lately."

"How do you figure that?" asked Sister.

Brother counted on his fingers. "There's Bonnie Brown, Bertha Broom, and Ferdy Factual."

Bonnie Brown was Squire Grizzly's niece. She moved back and forth between her uncle's mansion and her parents' house in the city, where she sometimes worked as a model. Ferdy Factual was Actual Factual's nephew. He lived a lot like Bonnie. He spent months at a time with his uncle and long periods off on expeditions with his scientist parents. In fact, only Bertha Broom had really moved to town for good. Cousin Freddy pointed this out to Brother and Sister.

"Which means," said Brother, "that the

only cub to actually move into the neighborhood lately is definitely a..."

"Girl," Sister admitted. "Okay, I guess it's
all right for the new cub to be a boy. I wonder what he'll be like."

"I hope he'll be like so tall," said Brother,
reaching up as high as he could. "I hope he
can jump out of the gym."

"But you've already got a center for the
basketball team," said Sister. She grinned.
"The lovely and charming Too-Tall Grizzly."

"Don't remind us," said Freddy. Freddy was team manager, and Brother played point guard.

"Yeah," said Brother. "Too-Tall has a lot of talent, but he's a selfish player. He hogs the ball. He won't pass off to anyone except Skuzz and Smirk. And he takes too many three-point shots. What's more, he plays dirty."

"Won't his mom wash his uniform for him?" asked Sister.

Brother started to explain that he didn't mean that kind of dirty. But when he saw that Sister was grinning, he knew she was just putting him on again. That was the trouble with Sister: you could never tell whether she was *playing* dumb or *being* dumb.

"And he's such a slick dirty player," said Fred.

"Right," said Brother. "He'll grab the seat of your pants when you're about to go up for a jump shot. And his idea of blocking out for a rebound is to stomp on your foot."

Sister shook her head. "I didn't know he was *that* bad," she said.

"He is," said Brother. "So I hope this

Harry McGill is a great big cub who can play circles around Too-Tall on the basketball court."

"You guys are going to have to get real lucky for that to happen," said Sister.

"We can always hope," said Freddy. "After all, who would have thought Bertha Broom would beat out Too-Tall at fullback on the *boys'* football team!"

The cubs came to the McGills' house. The McGills had not moved in yet. Carpenters were still busy working on the house, replacing rotten window frames and making other repairs. As the cubs passed the house, they saw that the front steps were being removed.

"They're probably rotten like the window frames," said Freddy.

"They don't look rotten to me," said Sister.

"How can you tell?" asked Freddy.

"Because my eyesight is twenty-twenty. And you're not wearing your glasses."

Freddy moved his glasses down from the top of his head. "Hey, you're right," he said. "Those steps don't look rotten at all. So why are they being replaced?"

"Beats me," said Sister.

Brother shrugged. "Me too."

Chapter 2
A Boy's Best Friend

At the very moment that Brother, Sister, and Cousin Freddy were passing the McGills' new house on Boxwood Drive, Mr. McGill was returning home from work to the McGills' old apartment far away in Big Bear City. Tomorrow was the day he and his family would move to the house on Boxwood Drive.

Mr. McGill worked for Squire Grizzly. He had just been promoted, and that meant that he would have a lot of meetings with Squire Grizzly at the Grizzly mansion. So he and his family were moving closer to the Grizzly mansion.

Mrs. McGill greeted her husband with a kiss. "You're home early," she said.

"Last day at the office," he said. "Did you forget?"

"No," said Mrs. McGill. "I just didn't know that it wouldn't be a full day."

"Yep," said Mr. McGill. He took off his suit jacket and loosened his tie. "After lunch all I had to do was clean out my desk and say good-bye to my friends."

"Speaking of friends," said Mrs. McGill, "can you take Harry to say his good-byes now?"

"Where is he? On the computer?"

Mrs. McGill nodded. Mr. McGill went quietly down the hall to his son's room and opened the door just enough to peek in. There sat Harry in his wheelchair in front of the computer. His fingers were flying over the keyboard. Mr. McGill closed the door and returned to the living room. "Harry's sure gotten to be a whiz on that thing," he said to his wife.

Mrs. McGill looked up from the magazine she was reading. "Too much of a whiz, if you ask me," she said.

"How do you mean?"

"He used to go to the rehabilitation center to play wheelchair basketball every week," said Mrs. McGill. "Now he spends so much time on the computer that he doesn't seem to have time for his friends anymore."

"But he bulletin-boards with cubs all over Bear Country on that thing," said Mr. McGill. "He plays chess with them too."

"Bulletin-boarding with strangers isn't the same as having friends, dear," said Mrs. McGill. "And playing chess across town by computer isn't the same as *being* with someone. Besides, only a couple of his chess friends are *real* friends."

"But his real friends are in wheelchairs just like he is," said Mr. McGill. "It's a lot of trouble for them to get around. No wonder they like to keep in touch by computer."

"Well, I don't think it's very healthy," said Mrs. McGill. "It isn't healthy never to be with other cubs or to have only other disabled cubs for friends. Harry's got to learn to get along with non-disabled cubs too."

"You're right, dear," said Mr. McGill. "But it isn't as if Harry hasn't tried to make friends with non-disabled cubs. You know what he says about that."

"I know," said Mrs. McGill with a sigh. "They stare at him and ask him how he got 'hurt.' And even when they act friendly, they don't want to be *real* friends. They'll talk to him at school, but they never invite him to parties or to the Burger Bear for milk shakes. I guess they just think he's too different from them to ever fit in. So they never really get to know him. And now he's given up trying to make friends with them."

Mrs. McGill looked up at her husband. "What's Harry going to do when he grows up and has to work with others? How many of his fellow workers will be in wheelchairs?"

"Well," said Mr. McGill, "at least things will be different out in the country. There aren't any other disabled cubs at Bear Country School. If Harry wants any friends at all, he'll *have* to make friends with nondisabled cubs."

"Or maybe he'll decide he doesn't want any friends at all," said Mrs. McGill gloomily. "Except for his computer."

Mr. McGill went to the window and looked out. "Hmm," he said. "I never

thought of that." He turned and went down the hall to Harry's room. From inside came the click of keyboard keys. He knocked on the door.

"Yeah?" called Harry.

Mr. McGill opened the door and leaned into the room.

Harry looked up for a moment from the monitor. "Hi, Dad," he said. "What's up?"

"I'm ready to take you in the van to say your good-byes."

Harry frowned. "But I've almost got Billy Black in checkmate," he said.

"You can sign off for now and finish the game after dinner," said his father.

"Couldn't I just type in a good-bye message after the game?"

"I think Billy would feel a lot better about it if you went to say good-bye in person," said Mr. McGill. "Besides, there must be other cubs you want to say good-bye to."

Harry typed a sign-off message to Billy and switched off the computer. He turned his wheelchair so that he was facing his father. "Well," he said, "there's Max Grizzinski. That's all."

Billy Black and Max Grizzinski were both disabled cubs. Mr. McGill had an urge to ask, "Are you sure there isn't anyone else?" But he thought better of it.

Chapter 3
A Warning from Mama

When Brother, Sister, and Cousin Freddy passed the house on Boxwood Drive again the next afternoon, they saw that the front steps had been replaced with a cement ramp.

"Hey," said Fred. "What do you suppose it's for?"

"Don't know," said Sister. "But whatever it's for, it would be great for roller-skating. Instead of putting on my skates outside, I'd put them on inside. Then I'd skate down that ramp and off I'd go!"

"I'd use it for skateboarding," said Freddy. "And maybe, in the winter, for sledding. What do *you* think it's for, Brother?"

Brother thought for a moment, then said, "I don't know. But I don't think it's for skating, sledding, or skateboarding. I'll ask Mama about it at dinner tonight. She'll know."

And she did. "I heard from Millie McGrizz that Harry McGill is disabled," said Mama. "That new ramp is there to help him get in and out of the house in his wheelchair."

The cubs were very quiet. Brother just said, "Gee." Sister didn't say anything at all. She stared off into space. She was busy thinking her own thoughts.

Mama could see that the cubs were shocked. She thought they were maybe even a little frightened about what she had just told them. She pictured Harry McGill's first day at Bear Country School and saw Brother and Sister staring at Harry as if he were something strange and scary. That would never do. Harry would not be able to make any friends that way. And the other cubs would miss out on getting to know him.

"Well, being in a wheelchair isn't so unusual," said Mama. "You've seen Barry Bruin's grandfather. He uses a wheelchair. And so does Miz McGrizz's sister, Nellie."

"That's different," said Brother.

"What's different about it?" asked Mama.

"Barry's grandfather and Nellie McGrizz are *old*," said Brother. "And Harry is *my* age. He has his whole life ahead of him!"

"Yes, that's true," said Mama. She tried to think of another way to talk about the subject.

Sister also sat thinking hard about something. Suddenly a hopeful look came into her eyes. "Maybe he'll get better," she said. "Maybe the doctors can fix him up."

"I...er, don't think they expect that to happen," said Mama.

The look on Brother's face changed from thoughtful to curious. "How did it happen?" he asked. "How did Harry get hurt?"

"I'm not sure," said Mama. "I think it was some sort of accident."

"What kind of accident?" asked Brother.

"A car accident?" asked Sister.

"A plane crash?" asked Brother.

"Maybe he fell off a cliff!" said Sister. "Maybe he got shot! Maybe..."

"Now hush!" said Mama.

"What did I say?" said Sister.

"It's both of you," said Mama. "You mustn't get carried away thinking about

Newspaper headlines shown in the illustration:

BEARCITY CUB ~ARENDED ON ~AMILY JAUNT

CUB SUFFERS ROUGH LANDING VISITING GRANDPAREN~

GROUND GIVES WAY AT EDGE OF SCENIC VIEW AS LOCAL CUB MOUNTS CLIFF

Harry's injury and his being in a wheelchair. It will be much better for everyone if you treat him just like any other cub."

"But he isn't just like any other cub," said Sister. "He can't walk!"

Mama looked at Papa. Papa shrugged. Mama sighed. It was hard to explain some things to cubs. "Trust me on this for now," said Mama. "We can discuss it more later. Now let's clear the dinner table."

But the cubs had a lot of homework that evening. So they never did get to continue their discussion with Mama. They did their homework in the living room while Papa sat in his easy chair reading the afternoon newspaper. But both cubs were still thinking about Harry McGill. That made it hard to concentrate.

Sister groaned when she came to her math homework. Now it wasn't just Harry McGill making it hard to concentrate. It was fractions too. She just didn't understand them.

Papa looked up from his paper. "What's the problem, Sister?" he asked.

"One-fifth," said Sister. She frowned down at her math book. "I know what *one* means and I know what *fifth* means. But when you put them together... I just don't get it."

24

"Hmm," said Papa. "What don't you get?"

"Well, there's *one* TV set in the room," she said. She pointed to the bookshelves and counted along the bottom shelf. "And I see the *fifth* book on the bottom shelf. But you can't get 'one-fifth' by putting the TV and the book together."

"No, you certainly can't," said Papa.

"You're talking about fractions. That's easy!"
He thought for a moment. "Now think
about that TV and forget the book. It's one
whole TV set, right?"

"Right," said Sister.

"Suppose you took that TV set apart,"
said Papa. "That would split up the whole
TV into parts. You'd have the TV tube.

You'd have all the wires, and the nuts and bolts...you'd have all sorts of stuff lying around...in fact, you'd have a big mess on your hands!" Papa frowned. "What was I talking about?"

"Fractions," said Brother without even looking up from his own math homework.

"Oh, yes. So we started with one whole TV set, and we ended up with a big mess of TV parts...and..." Papa's voiced trailed off. He frowned again and scratched his head. "Hmm..."

"Think of the book and forget the TV, Sis," said Brother. "Suppose that book had a hundred pages. And suppose you took each twenty pages and paper-clipped them together. Then you'd have five equal parts of twenty pages each. Each of those five parts is one-fifth of the book."

Sister's frown broke into a smile. "So

twenty is one-fifth of a hundred!" she cried.

"Exactly," said Brother. "You've got it."

Papa chuckled. Then he was quiet for a moment. "I had it too," he said. "I mean, I use fractions all the time in my work, measuring boards and stuff. I just couldn't explain it. Never was any good at explaining things like that."

"I guess that's why you didn't become a teacher, Papa," said Sister.

"Well, you're right, in a way," said Papa. "When I was your age, I used to think about becoming a teacher someday. I've always admired people who could explain things. But I wound up becoming a carpenter instead."

"But you're a very *good* carpenter," said Sister.

"Best in Bear Country!" Papa smiled and gave Sister a little hug.

Mama came in from the kitchen. "As soon as your homework is done, it'll be time to get ready for bed, cubs," she said.

After finishing their homework, the cubs got into their pajamas and brushed their teeth. Papa read Sister a bedtime story. Brother thought he was too old for bedtime stories. But that didn't stop him from listening.

Then Mama came upstairs to tuck them

in. Brother had already fallen asleep. Mama kissed her sleeping cub gently on the forehead. But Sister was still wide-awake. Mama could see that she had something important on her mind.

"A penny for your thoughts," said Mama. She sat on the bed beside Sister.

"Maybe I could just ask him," said Sister. She stared at the ceiling.

"Maybe you could just ask who what?"

"Harry McGill," said Sister. "Maybe I could just ask him how he got hurt."

"You'll do no such thing!" said Mama. "And if I hear that you did... Well, just don't do it." She smoothed the covers and kissed Sister on the forehead. "Now close your eyes."

"Okay, okay," said Sister. She pulled the covers up to her chin and closed her eyes as Mama quietly left the room.

Chapter 4
Off to a Bad Start

The next morning, the cubs of Bear Country School were gathered in the schoolyard. They were waiting for the bell to start the school day. Sister and Brother Bear were talking with Queenie McBear and Babs Bruno near the dodgeball court. Suddenly Queenie looked up and pointed to a blue van that had stopped at the front gate.

"Whose van is that?" she asked.

"I don't know," said Babs.

"I've never seen it before," said Brother.

The driver got out and pulled open the side panel of the van. The cubs watched as a boy cub in a wheelchair was lowered to the ground on a movable platform that was attached to the side of the van.

"That must be the new cub, Harry McGill," said Sister. "He's disabled."

"He sure is!" said Queenie, staring. "He's going to need a lot of help from the rest of us—a *lot* of help."

"Er...I don't know about that," said Sister. "Mama said we should treat Harry just like any other cub."

Queenie looked at Sister with surprise. "Why?" she asked. "I mean, just *look* at him!" Queenie was the sort of cub who plunged into things. She didn't take "maybe" for an answer.

HE'S GOING TO NEED A **LOT** OF HELP!

Harry did not join the other cubs in the schoolyard. Instead, he wheeled himself toward the side door. He stared straight ahead.

"What's with him?" said Babs. "Why would a cub in a wheelchair act stuck-up like that?"

"I don't think he's acting stuck-up," said Brother. "The school built a little wooden ramp at the side door. Harry's got to use it to get in."

"But why didn't he come meet some of us other cubs *before* he went to the side door?" said Babs. "Why doesn't he wait for the bell with the rest of us—JUST LIKE ANY OTHER CUB?" Babs glared at Sister.

Sister blushed. "I don't know," she said. "You'd have to ask *him* that." Then quickly she added, "But don't!"

The morning bell rang and the cubs went

to their classrooms. As Brother, Babs, and Queenie entered Teacher Bob's class, they saw Harry McGill sitting in the far corner at the back of the room. His wheelchair made an extra seat in the back row.

If Sister and Queenie had thought about it, they would have known why Harry wanted to get to class before the other cubs. But Sister wasn't in Harry's class. Besides, she had problems of her own. Fractions, for instance.

As for Queenie, thinking wasn't exactly her middle name. But if Sister and Queenie had been in Harry's place, they would have understood. The stares and whispers of the other cubs entering the room were bad enough. But it would have been much worse if Harry had to make a grand entrance in his wheelchair with everyone else already in their seats!

Queenie noticed some of the cubs staring at Harry. Even Queenie knew it was rude to stare. "Look at that!" she said to Brother. "That's no way to treat a new cub! I'm going to go over to Harry right now and make him feel really welcome."

"Er, wait a minute, Queenie...," said Brother.

But Queenie was already on her way. She walked right up to the new cub and held out her hand. "Hi, Harry!" she said loudly.

Everyone turned around to look. "I'm Queenie McBear. I want to welcome you to Bear Country School. If you ever need any help—a little push, a little lift—just whistle and I'll be there in a flash!"

Harry shook Queenie's hand. He looked down at the floor. "Uh, thanks," he mumbled. "But I don't really...need...much help." He blushed and turned to look out the window.

Leave it to Queenie, thought Brother.

Queenie returned to her seat. She leaned over to Brother and said with a wink, "He pretended he doesn't need help. Just being polite, I guess."

"I don't think he was pretending," said Brother. "And I don't think he was being polite, either. I think he was *embarrassed*."

"Oh, don't be silly," said Queenie. "Why would anyone be embarrassed by someone trying to make friends?"

Just then Teacher Bob clapped his hands.

IN THE WHEELCHAIR!

"May I have your attention, class," he said. "Before we begin today, I'd like to introduce our newest student, Harry McGill. Harry's the one in the...er, uh...back row." Some of the cubs giggled. Teacher Bob coughed nervously. "Harry, would you raise your hand so the cubs will know...uh...which one...you are...."

There were more giggles.

"They already know which one I am," said Harry coldly. "I'm the one—as you were about to say—IN THE WHEEL-CHAIR!"

The class fell silent. They had never seen Teacher Bob blush before.

Teacher Bob coughed again and cleared his throat. He wanted to help Harry, not embarrass him. But somehow he kept saying embarrassing things.

"Er, Harry," he said, "maybe you'd like to

sit closer to the blackboard. There's room right up here..."

"No thanks," said Harry.

"It really wouldn't be any trouble—"

"NO THANKS," said Harry again. "Just because I can't use my legs doesn't mean I can't see."

The silence in the classroom was even deeper this time. Teacher Bob blushed an even deeper shade of red. "Er...uh...," he said.

Then, to Teacher Bob's great relief, he remembered an important announcement. "Oh, yes!" he said. "I'm very pleased to announce that Squire Grizzly has given our school six personal computers. They will be set up in a special new computer room. We could use your help with this, class. You see, neither I nor any of the other teachers know anything about computers. I tried to learn about them a while back. But to tell you the truth, I just couldn't seem to get the hang of it. Do any of you know enough about computers to help us get our computer center rolling?" Oops! There I go again, thought Teacher Bob. "Er, I mean, started."

Dead silence filled the room. Harry McGill sat quietly with his arms folded across his chest. No one raised a hand. Including Harry.

"Well," said Teacher Bob. He cleared his throat again. "I guess we'd better move on to English. But if anyone knows of someone who could be of help with the computers, please stay behind for a minute after I dismiss the class for recess."

Harry McGill was the only cub who stayed behind. But it wasn't because he wanted to help Teacher Bob with the new computers. As the rest of the class filed noisily out of the room, Harry sat right where he was. He didn't move a muscle.

Teacher Bob looked up from the lesson plans on his desk. "Harry," he said. "Is there something I can do for you?"

"No, I'm fine," said Harry.

"But it's time for recess. And you're still here."

"That's right," said Harry.

"Why?"

"I don't feel like going," said Harry.

"But the other cubs want to meet you and get to know you."

"Baloney," said Harry.

Teacher Bob's eyebrows raised. "Did I hear you correctly, Harry?"

"The other cubs may want to meet me," said Harry. "But they *don't* want to get to know me. They just want to find out how...you know...how I got disabled. After that, they'll forget all about me."

"But if you just give them a chance..."

"Forget it," said Harry. "I've been through this before."

Teacher Bob sighed. "Well, I'm sorry you feel that way, Harry," he said. "But you're going to have to join the other cubs at recess. School rules. Every student must attend recess unless..." Teacher Bob stopped short.

"Unless what?" said Harry.

"Never mind," said Teacher Bob. He was blushing again.

"I should learn the school rules," said Harry. "Unless what?"

Teacher Bob took a deep breath. "Unless physically unable," he said softly.

Harry's eyes narrowed. He clenched his jaw. "Don't worry," he said. "I'm able!"

With powerful strokes of his muscular arms, Harry wheeled himself across the room and out the door.

Teacher Bob sighed again as he watched Harry go. It's a good thing Too-Tall and the gang are still suspended, he thought. They'd embarrass that poor cub a lot more than I did. And they'd do it on purpose.

Chapter 5
Queenie Goofs Again

At recess, Harry parked his wheelchair under an elm tree near the schoolyard fence. He spoke to no one. None of the cubs tried to speak to him, either. Some of them just weren't interested in meeting Harry. Others were curious about him, but they remembered how he had treated Teacher Bob in class. They were afraid that Harry would snap at them if they tried to talk to him.

Sister was one of the curious ones. And Mama's strict orders just made her more curious about what had happened to Harry. Being curious was sort of like having an itch you couldn't scratch. So Sister went looking for Brother. She asked him if anyone had asked Harry how he had become disabled.

"Nope," said Brother. "And I wouldn't want to be the one who tried it. He's a pretty touchy guy. When Teacher Bob tried to be helpful in class, Harry just about bit his head off. Uh-oh. There goes Queenie again. What's she up to now?"

"Hey, Harry," Queenie was saying. "All the cubs are wondering about something. So can I ask you a question?"

"You can ask," said Harry.

"Well, what we were wondering about is how you got crippled—er, I mean, hurt."

Harry glared at Queenie for a moment. Then he wheeled his wheelchair around and headed for the side door. He moved with surprising speed. He went smoothly up the ramp, but he had trouble opening the door.

Queenie hurried after him. "Hey, let me give you a hand!..."

"No thanks!" growled Harry. With his strong arms, he finally got the door opened and slipped inside.

Queenie saw Brother and Sister watching. She came over to them with a puzzled look on her face. "What did I say?" she asked. "What did I say?"

Brother was about to bawl Queenie out, but he decided not to. Queenie couldn't help it if she had a big mouth.

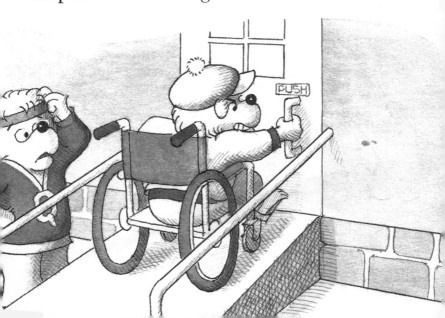

Chapter 6
Report Card

That afternoon Mr. McGill picked Harry up at school. "Hi, son," he said cheerfully when Harry reached the van. But Harry didn't answer.

"Who was that girl who waved good-bye to you?" asked Mr. McGill as they drove away from the crowded schoolyard.

"Oh, her," said Harry with a big frown. "That was Queenie McBear."

"She seems friendly," said Mr. McGill.

Oh boy, thought Harry. Here we go again. We're not even a hundred yards from school and already Dad wants to know if I made friends with any of the "*normal*" cubs. "*Too* friendly, if you ask me," he said. "And too curious."

Mr. McGill sighed. "Did she ask...THE question?"

"Of course," said Harry. "Don't they always? She even used the 'c' word, then changed it to 'hurt.'"

"Well, what about Teacher Bob?" asked Mr. McGill. "What's he like?"

"Too helpful," said Harry.

"What did he do?"

"I sat in the back row in the corner so I would only get stares from one direction. So Teacher Bob asked me if I wanted to move closer to the blackboard," said Harry.

"And you said that you couldn't walk but you could see fine, or something like that," said Mr. McGill.

Harry didn't answer.

"You know, son," said Mr. McGill, "it just might be that Teacher Bob asks that of *every* new student who sits in the back row. Did you ever think of that?"

"No," said Harry. "Because it isn't so."

Mr. McGill sighed again and said nothing more. It was so hard to talk to Harry about these things. As usual, his son's mind seemed to be made up.

Chapter 7
Brother and Sister Catch On

Not long after Harry and his dad reached the house on Boxwood Drive, Brother and Sister Bear arrived at their tree house. Brother wanted to save the subject of Harry

McGill for dinner-table conversation. But Sister couldn't wait to tell Mama what she had seen at recess. She dashed ahead of Brother and up the front steps and into the kitchen.

"Mama!" she said. "You were right!"

"About what?" asked Mama as she dipped a large wooden spoon into the fish stew she was cooking for dinner.

"About Harry McGill," said Sister. She told Mama about Queenie's question at recess and about how angry Harry had been. "Brother says that before recess Harry got mad at Queenie and Teacher Bob for trying to help him," Sister added. "I don't understand that."

Mama asked Brother if Queenie and

Teacher Bob had offered to help Harry because of his disability.

"Queenie did," said Brother. "But I'm not so sure about Teacher Bob. It kind of looked that way, though. And he'd already embarrassed Harry in class by mentioning the wheelchair. Or *almost* mentioning the wheelchair, I guess."

"Well, there you have it," said Mama.

"Have *what?*" asked Sister.

"Think about it," said Mama. "Suppose every time someone spoke to Papa they said something about his never becoming a teacher."

"Who cares about that?" said Sister. "Papa became a great carpenter!"

"That's right," said Mama. "And suppose everyone kept reminding *you* about something you can't do very well."

"Like what?" asked Sister.

53

"Well, like having a hard time with math," said Mama.

"But I'm good at all kinds of things!" cried Sister. "Science, English, history, baseball, hopscotch, jump rope, roller-skating, dancing!... It wouldn't be fair if people kept reminding me about math!"

Mama smiled. "Exactly," she said.

"Exactly what?" asked Sister. "What's it have to do with Harry McGill?"

"It has everything to do with Harry McGill," said Mama. "Everyone must do that very thing to him all the time. When they meet him for the first time, they ask or say something about the most obvious thing he can't do—walk. And they probably don't give a moment's thought to the things he *can* do."

"But nobody knows what he *can* do," said Sister.

"And you'll never find out if you all keep worrying about why he can't walk," said Mama.

Sister's face suddenly lit up. So did Brother's. "Oh!" they said together. "I get it!"

"Well, I'm glad to hear that," said Mama.

"I know what I'll do!" said Sister. "Tomorrow I'll go right up to Harry and ask him what he's good at!"

"Wait just a minute now," said Mama. "You'll do no such thing."

"Why not?" said Sister.

"It sounds as if Harry had a hard first day at school," said Mama. "I'll bet he'll be in a pretty bad mood when he gets to school tomorrow. So be patient. Give him a day or two to cool off."

"Tomorrow could be a lot worse for Harry than today was," said Brother. "Too-Tall and the gang will be back from suspension. It looks like Harry could be in for a rough time."

"I'm sure Harry has had to deal with bullies before," said Mama. "I just hope he'll be ready this time."

"Don't worry," said Brother. "If Too-Tall goes after Harry, I'll tell him off good!"

"Well, I guess that's all right," said Mama. "I know how you hate to see Too-Tall bully other cubs. But don't make too big a deal of it."

"Why not?" asked Brother.

"Because Harry might think you're sticking up for him just because he's disabled," said Mama. "Or that you're using his troubles just to show off to your friends."

"Hmm," said Brother. "I see what you mean. We'll be cool about it. Won't we, Sis? Sis?"

But Sister wasn't listening. She was deep in thought. Suddenly her eyes lit up again. "I know!" she said. "I'll tell Harry that I think it's really cool that he can't walk and uses a wheelchair!"

Brother rolled his eyes and groaned.

"What's wrong with that?" asked Sister.

"Harry may not be able to walk, Sis," said Brother. "But that doesn't mean he's STUPID."

Chapter 8
Card Game

The next morning, at the start of recess, Harry McGill did not stay away from the other cubs. In fact, he went up to each of them and gave them something.

Sister Bear and Lizzy Bruin were playing jump rope. Suddenly Sister stopped and asked, "What's Harry handing out?"

"They look like cards of some sort," said Lizzy. "Shush—here he comes."

Harry moved toward the girls. He wasn't smiling and he wasn't frowning. He had no

expression at all on his face. He calmly handed them each a small piece of white paper shaped like a business card. Then he went on his way.

Sister looked down at the card. On it was printed "For the information of all nosy cubs who don't know how to mind their own business: I was injured in a car accident four years ago." It was signed "Harry (The Cripple) McGill."

"If this is supposed to be some kind of a joke, I don't get it," said Lizzy.

"It's no joke," said Sister. "Harry must still be upset about Queenie asking him how he got hurt."

"He sure has a weird way of showing it," said Lizzy. "Why doesn't he just go up to Queenie and call her some names?"

Just then Brother came up behind them. "Something tells me Harry isn't into name-calling," he said. "He must have been called some pretty nasty names in his day."

"Where do you guys think he got these?" asked Sister, looking at the card in her hand.

"The printing looks like it was made by a computer printer," said Lizzy.

"Yeah," said Brother. "And the edges

For the information of all nosy cubs who don't know how to mind their own business: I was injured in a car accident four years ago. Harry (The Cripple) McGill

aren't exactly straight. I think someone used a computer to print bunches of these onto sheets of computer paper. Then they cut up the sheets into card-size pieces with a scissors. Hmm. Do you think Harry..."

"Has a computer?" asked Sister.

"Exactly," said Brother.

"That'd be neat," said Sister. "Someone had better tell Teacher Bob. I hear he's looking for help with the new computer center."

"Just what I was thinking," said Brother. "Funny, Harry didn't say anything yesterday when Teacher Bob mentioned it."

When the bell rang for lunch, Teacher Bob called Too-Tall to the front of the classroom. Too-Tall stomped up to Teacher Bob and said, "What'd I do now?" Skuzz, Smirk, and Vinnie followed and stood behind their leader.

"The rest of you guys are dismissed," said Teacher Bob.

When the gang didn't move, Too-Tall turned to them and yelled, "You heard the man! Wait for me in the hall, you bums!"

As the gang left, Too-Tall gave Teacher Bob a big grin. "You gotta know how to sweet-talk those guys, Teach," he said.

"Let's get to the point," said Teacher Bob. "What have you got in your pocket?"

"My pocket?" said Too-Tall. He reached into his left pants pocket and drew out something small and shiny. "You mean my new hand-buzzer? Didn't know you were into those kinds of things, Teach." He put the buzzer in the palm of his hand and held his hand out. "Wanna give it a try? Here, shake!"

"Some other time," said Teacher Bob. "I'm talking about the little white card you

HERE, SHAKE!

took out and snickered at with Skuzz while I was trying to teach you geometry."

"Oh, *that*," said Too-Tall. "You didn't say *which* pocket." From his right pocket, he produced Harry's McGill's card. "Here you go, Teach."

As Teacher Bob read the card, a frown came across his face. "What are you doing with this?" he asked.

"Hey, it ain't just me, Teach," said Too-Tall. "Everybody's got 'em. That crippled kid passed 'em out at recess."

"Did you say the word 'crippled' to Harry?" asked Teacher Bob.

"Nah, but I hear Queenie did. Why?"

"It's not the best word to use for a disabled bear," said Teacher Bob.

"What's wrong with it? He *is* crippled, ain't he?"

"It isn't just what the word *means* that's important," said Teacher Bob. "How it's said matters too. For years the words 'cripple' and 'crippled' have been used in unfriendly ways. Now disabled bears are sick of hearing them."

"Thanks, Teach," said Too-Tall. "I'll be sure to use them when I meet this cripple."

"You'll do no such thing!" snapped Teacher Bob. "I should have known better than to waste a good explanation on you, Too-Tall. If I hear anything about you and the gang bothering Harry at lunch or recess, I'll see that you're suspended again. You're dismissed."

"Gee, thanks for the advice, Teach," said Too-Tall sweetly. With a snicker, he turned and strutted out to the hallway to join his gang.

Chapter 9
The Breakthrough

At the end of the day, as Brother Bear and Cousin Freddy were leaving Bear Country School, they were surprised to see Harry McGill hurrying toward them from the side door. He stopped right in front of them. He was blocking their path to the front gate. He looked Brother right in the eye.

"We need to talk," he said.

Cubs were streaming around them as they poured out of the building.

"Okay," said Brother. "But maybe we should move first. We're blocking the way."

"Let 'em go around us," said Harry.

"Have it your way," said Brother. "What's up?"

"Remember when Teacher Bob came to the back of the classroom to talk to me while we were doing our spelling exercises?" asked Harry.

"Yeah, I guess so."

"Of course you do," said Harry. "*Everybody* turned around to stare at us."

"Okay, I remember."

"Teacher Bob asked me to help set up the new computer center," said Harry. "He said you told him that I know a lot about computers."

"I said I thought you *might* know a lot about computers," said Brother. "I figured it out from those cards you passed out."

"My mistake," said Harry. "I never should have printed up those cards. Anyway, from now on, do me a favor. Mind your own business. I don't need special attention from Teacher Bob or anyone else. Understand?"

Brother looked wide-eyed at Harry. He didn't know what to say. He hadn't tried to get Teacher Bob to give Harry special attention. He just wanted to help the computer center. Harry was being so unfair!

"Well, gotta run," said Harry. "Or would you rather I said 'roll'?" He turned toward the gate, where Mr. McGill had just pulled up in the blue van.

But before Harry could move, Too-Tall and the gang surrounded him. "What's happenin', cripple?" sneered Too-Tall. "Oops, I

forgot—Teacher Bob says we're not supposed to call you that. What should we call him instead, gang?"

"How about *Wheels?*" said Skuzz. Smirk and Vinnie snickered.

"Wheels," said Too-Tall. "I like the sound of that."

"Hey," teased Vinnie, "you're hassling Wheels!"

"So?" said Too-Tall.

"So Teacher Bob said you ain't allowed to hassle him."

"He said I'm not allowed to hassle him at *lunch* and *recess*," replied Too-Tall. "He didn't say a word about *after school*."

"Oooh, I'm gonna tell Teacher Bob on you, Too-Tall," said Smirk in a mocking voice.

Too-Tall pretended to be hurt. He screwed up his face as if he were about to

cry. "Cut it out, you bullies!" he whined. "You're always pickin' on me! *I'm* gonna tell Teacher Bob on *you* guys! *He'll* protect me, just like he protects Wheels here. And I'll tell my dad to pick me up after school like Wheels here so *he* can protect me too..."

Brother got angrier and angrier as he listened to the gang hassle Harry. Finally he'd had enough. He stepped between Harry and Too-Tall and raised a fist at Too-Tall. "You're asking for a knuckle sandwich," he said.

"No, I ain't," said Too-Tall. "I already had lunch."

"Since when did Mama and Papa Bear teach you to solve problems with violence, Brother?" said Skuzz.

"Since he started hangin' around with his nerdy cousin here," said Smirk. "The poor nerd needs all the protection he can get."

"Shut up!" screamed Freddy. "Don't call me that!"

"Who's gonna make us?" said Vinnie.

"Cool it, guys," said Too-Tall. "I've got better things to do than stand here wearing my jaw out over Brother Bear's crippled new buddy. Let's go get our bikes and ride down to the Burger Bear for milk shakes. Wanna come along, Wheels? We can all do some wheelies on the way!"

The gang strutted off to the schoolyard gate, laughing and joking as they went.

"Don't pay any attention to them," Brother told Harry. "They're just a bunch of jerks."

Harry was red-faced with anger. But not because of Too-Tall and the gang. "Didn't I just get finished telling you to mind your own business?" he growled. "I don't need special protection because I'm disabled!"

At first the force of Harry's anger surprised Brother. "But...I didn't mean...," he stammered. Then, all of a sudden, he got

very angry with Harry. He wasn't going to let Harry talk that way to him just because he was disabled! Brother folded his arms across his chest and glared down at Harry. "Look, jerk," he said. "I didn't stick up for you because you're disabled. I stick up for *everybody* who gets bullied by that big creep!"

Harry was startled. He looked up at Brother. This cub seems to mean what he's saying, thought Harry. But he still wasn't sure he could believe it.

"I'll vouch for that," said Freddy.

"Brother's famous around here for standing up to Too-Tall. Last spring he even picked Too-Tall up and put him in a Dumpster at the mall when he was giving Bonnie Brown a hard time."

Harry's eyes grew wide. "Oh, come on," he said. "You're putting me on."

"No way," said Freddy. "It's the truth. I swear."

Harry looked at Brother again. "You really did that?" he asked.

"Sure," said Brother. He was still angry. "I did it for Bonnie Brown. But I *wouldn't* do it for *you.*"

For the first time since coming to Bear Country School, Harry McGill smiled. "Guess I had you wrong," he said. "You're okay. Both of you."

Brother and Freddy were so surprised to see Harry smile, they forgot all about being angry with him. They smiled back.

"Thanks," said Brother. "No harm done. Well, guess we'd better get going."

"Hey, wait," said Harry. "Why don't you guys come over to my house. I'll show you my computer. You can ride with me and my dad."

"How about meeting us at the park instead," said Brother. "Freddy and I have some testing to do on my new remote-control model airplane. We haven't been able to get its center of gravity right."

"I can help with that," said Harry. "I love airplanes. I've got a great computer program all about them. If you'll bring your model over, I'll have a look at it and run some computer tests. I'll bet we can fix your center-of-gravity problem in no time."

"Great!" said Brother. "We'll go get the plane and come over."

Harry wheeled himself toward the van. "Boxwood Drive," he called over his shoulder. "You can't miss it. There's a big ramp in front."

A little way down the street, Too-Tall and the gang had stopped to watch. Too-Tall's eyes widened and his mouth hung open. "What's going on?" he said. "I thought that cripple didn't have any friends!"

"Looks like he does now, boss," said Skuzz.

Chapter 10
The Challenge

It took just ten minutes of work on his computer for Harry to solve Brother's airplane problem. When Brother saw what a computer whiz Harry was, he thought of asking Harry to change his mind about helping Teacher Bob with the computer center. But he decided not to bring it up. Something told him that just making new friends might help Harry change his mind about helping Bear Country School.

That's exactly what happened. The next morning, Harry went to Teacher Bob and volunteered to help organize and run the new computer center. Teacher Bob was delighted. And as it turned out, so were the cubs of Bear Country School. Harry

became the main after-school computer-center assistant. Cubs came to him for help with their computer problems. Soon they saw Harry as more than someone who couldn't walk. They saw him as a computer expert.

As the days passed, Harry made a lot of new friends. *Real* friends, not just cubs who said "hi" every morning and opened doors for him. They invited Harry to parties, to the park, to the Burger Bear for milk shakes. They got to know Harry as a computer expert, a great chess player, a lover of pop music, and a collector of old comedy videos of W. C. Bruin. The better they got to know him, the less they thought about his physical handicap.

But Harry's problems at school were not over yet. There were still four cubs who saw him as just a disabled cub. Their names were Too-Tall, Skuzz, Smirk, and Vinnie.

Too-Tall was secretly jealous of Harry's newfound popularity. To make matters worse, the nickname "Wheels" hadn't stuck to Harry in the nasty way Too-Tall had intended. In fact, Harry decided he *liked* the new nickname. He even asked everyone at school to call him Wheels! That only made Too-Tall madder.

"Forget about Too-Tall and the gang," Brother told Harry one day at recess, after a morning of the gang's teasing. "They just don't realize that *everybody's* got a handicap, even them."

"How do you mean?" asked Harry.

"My papa has a hard time explaining homework problems to Sister and me," said Brother. "Teacher Bob has trouble with computers. Sister has to study extra hard to do well in math. Freddy's no good at sports. And I'm a klutzy dancer. Our handicaps just aren't as easy to spot as yours."

"Hmm," said Harry. "I never thought of it that way. But what about Too-Tall and the gang? What's their handicap?"

"I guess Skuzz, Smirk, and Vinnie's handicap is that they feel like they need a leader every minute of the day," said Brother. "So they let Too-Tall boss them around all the time. And Too-Tall's handicap is that he's such a jerk."

Harry thought for a moment. "You're right about one thing and wrong about another," he said. "You're right about everyone having a handicap. But you're wrong about Too-Tall not realizing it. He realizes it as well as any cub I ever met. He figures out each cub's weak spot. Then he zeroes in on it and goes after them about it. The bigger the handicap, the harder he goes after them."

"You've got a point there," said Brother. "But there's still one very important thing Too-Tall doesn't know about handicaps."

"What's that?" asked Harry.

"That being a jerk is the biggest handicap of all."

"Right on, Brother," said Harry. He noticed that Brother kept glancing over at the basketball court. Too-Tall and the gang were playing four on four against a team led by Barry Bruin. "Want to go watch the game?" asked Harry.

"Nah," said Brother. "I'll stay here with you."

"We'll both go."

"You sure?" asked Brother. "Too-Tall will just start giving you a hard time."

Harry had a funny look in his eyes. "Let him," he said. "I just had a great idea."

"What is it?" asked Brother.

"We need modems at the computer center, but there's no money left in the budget. I just thought of a way to raise that money and teach Too-Tall a major lesson at the same time."

"How?" asked Brother.

"You'll see," said Harry.

They joined the other cubs at courtside. But the game had just ended. Too-Tall's team had beaten Barry Bruin's team by a score of twenty to two.

"Aw, come on, Barry," Too-Tall was saying. "Let's go again."

"No thanks," said Barry. "We'd just lose again."

"What're ya? *Chicken?*"

Skuzz, Smirk, and Vinnie started prancing around the court making chicken wings with their arms and going, "BAWK BAWK BAWK BAWK...!"

BAWK! BAWK!

Just then Too-Tall spotted Harry. "Hey, Wheels!" he called. "Wanna play?"

"Cool it, Too-Tall," said Barry.

"I'm serious!" said Too-Tall. "Wheels can take Vinnie's place. That'll give us a *handicap*—ha ha ha! If you turn down *this* challenge, Barry, then you're *really* chicken!"

"BAWK BAWK BAWK...!" went the gang.

Too-Tall didn't really expect Harry to play. But he was sure having a ball teasing him. "What do you say, Wheels?" he said. "You've gotten real popular around here all of a sudden. I'll bet your fans would like to see what you can do on the basketball court. Me and Skuzz and Smirk will even lift you up to the rim so you can show 'em all a slam dunk!"

The other cubs began to take Harry's side. "Cool it," someone said. "Yeah, cut it out, Too-Tall," said another.

But to everyone's great surprise, Harry wheeled himself right up to Too-Tall at center court and said, "Okay, I'll play."

Too-Tall looked down at Harry and grinned a wicked grin. He had visions of Harry's wheelchair getting turned this way and that and every which way. He'd make Harry look like a fool! "Great!" he said. "Let's get started!"

"Hold your horses," said Harry. "I'll play all right. But not now. And not as part of your team."

"So where?" asked Too-Tall. "And how?"

"One week from today, after school," said Harry. "One on one. Just you and me."

Too-Tall stared down at Harry for a sec-

ond. Then he burst into laughter. "You gotta be kiddin'!" he cried. "You and me? One on one? Have you lost your marbles, Wheels? I'll dribble circles around you! I'll block every shot!"

"No, you won't," said Harry calmly. "Because we're not going to play regular basketball. We're going to play *wheelchair* basketball."

"Hunh? Wheelchair basketball?"

"Yeah," said Harry. "We'll both be in wheelchairs."

"Come off it, Wheels," Too-Tall snorted. "I don't own a wheelchair."

"No problem," said Harry. "I've got two of them. I'll lend you one."

Too-Tall didn't answer.

"You can come over and get it after

school," said Harry. "That'll give you a whole week to practice."

The crowd of cubs was silent. Would Too-Tall accept Harry's challenge?

"What's the matter, Too-Tall?" asked Harry quietly but loud enough for everyone to hear. *"Chicken?"* He smiled, raised his eyebrows, did a few slow chicken wings with his arms, and said just as quietly, "Bawk bawk bawk?"

Too-Tall's face turned as red as a ripe tomato. The crowd gasped. They had never seen Too-Tall blush before. A few of them went, "BAWK BAWK BAWK!"

"Shut up, all of ya!" roared Too-Tall. The crowd went silent. Too-Tall glared down at Harry. "I've had enough of yer insults, Wheels," he snarled. "As far as I'm con-cerned, you're nothin' but a *cripple*. And you couldn't beat me at *anything*, whether it's wheelchair basketball, wheelchair water polo, or wheelchair tiddlywinks! I'll be over to pick up that wheelchair after school. And *you* better be there!"

With that, Too-Tall turned and stormed off the court. His gang followed.

"Listen up, cubs!" shouted Harry to the crowd. "Tickets go on sale tomorrow at the computer center for next week's Wheelchair Battle of the Century! All proceeds will go to the computer center for new equipment!"

Harry wheeled himself back to Brother's side. He was grinning from ear to ear. "Guess I showed Too-Tall, eh?" he said.

"I don't know," said Brother, shaking his head. "It kind of depends on what happens next week. If you lose, Too-Tall will never let you forget it. And he *is* the best athlete in the whole school."

"The best athlete *with normal, healthy legs*," Harry corrected. "Take his legs away and he's nothing!" Harry chuckled. "You walking cubs see a wheelchair and think there's nothing to it. Let me tell you, it isn't as easy as it looks. *Especially* on a basketball court."

"But Too-Tall's got a whole week to practice," Brother pointed out.

Harry chuckled again. "I used to play in the wheelchair basketball league in Big Bear City," he said. "There isn't a single cub in this school who could beat me at wheelchair basketball—even if he practiced *for a whole month*!"

"Well," said Brother. "For your sake, I hope you're right."

"For my sake," said Harry, "I hope we can get the school's permission to sell those tickets tomorrow!"

Chapter 11
The Battle of the Century

Getting permission to sell tickets to the Wheelchair Battle of the Century turned out to be no problem at all. Mr. Honeycomb, Bear Country School's principal, loved the idea. He even let Harry, Brother, and Freddy use the school's equipment to print up the tickets. The tickets went on sale that afternoon at the computer center and sold out in just a half-hour!

On the afternoon of the big one-on-one game, a large crowd of cubs gathered at the basketball court after school. Harry, Brother, Sister, and Cousin Freddy waited together at courtside.

"Wow," said Brother. "Look at this crowd.

We must have sold enough tickets to buy a cartload of modems. I think every cub in the school is here!"

"All except for one," said Sister, looking around.

"Who's missing?" asked Freddy.

"A cub by the name of Too-Tall Grizzly," said Sister.

"Do you suppose he chickened out?" said Brother. "He'd never live it down."

"Nah," said Harry. "He just wants to be

late enough to make a grand entrance with everyone watching."

Harry was exactly right. Moments later, Too-Tall appeared down the street, rolling along the sidewalk toward the front gate of the schoolyard. The crowd began to murmur.

"He's moving really well in that thing," said Cousin Freddy in a worried voice.

"Looks like he's been practicing," said Brother.

"Yeah," said Harry cheerfully. "Looks like he's gotten real good at rolling down the sidewalk in a straight line. Just wait till he

gets on the court. It'll be a different story."

Skuzz, Smirk, and Vinnie cheered wildly as Too-Tall entered the schoolyard and rolled to center court.

"Well, good luck, Wheels," said Cousin Freddy.

"Go get him, Wheels," said Brother.

The crowd cheered loudly as Harry moved forward to meet Too-Tall. It was to be a full-court game to a score of twenty.

Barry Bruin held the ball up for the opening tipoff. He tossed it in the air. Since it was a one-on-one game, the players tried to get control of the ball when it came down instead of trying to tip it to a teammate.

With his long arms and great height—even sitting down—Too-Tall was able to snatch the ball high above his head. But the instant he brought it down to dribble, Harry knocked it away with a lightning-fast slap of the hand.

The ball bounced toward Harry's basket. As Too-Tall went into an uncontrolled spin trying to get his wheelchair going, Harry zipped around him and headed downcourt at breakneck speed. He scooped up the ball near the foul line, dribbled to the basket, and laid the ball in off the backboard. The crowd cheered.

"Two points!" cried Sister. "Yahoo!"

"Great play!" yelled Brother.

"Go, Wheels!" screamed Freddy.

On the next play, Too-Tall came dribbling downcourt easily. But as soon as Harry rolled to meet him, Too-Tall dribbled the ball off one of his wheels. Again Harry raced after the loose ball, snatched it up, and laid it in. Four to nothing. The crowd roared.

Too-Tall was simply no match for Harry. The score mounted. Eight to nothing. Twelve to nothing. The crowd roared again and again as Harry made dazzling plays and Too-Tall's wheelchair got turned every which way but the right way.

Soon it was eighteen to nothing. Harry had the ball. One more basket and the game would be over. Harry looked as fresh as when the game had started. Too-Tall was dripping with sweat and dizzy from all his crazy wheelchair spins.

Harry came dribbling swiftly downcourt and headed right down the lane toward the basket. At the last second, he gave Too-Tall a head fake. Too-Tall lurched to block the imaginary shot and went sprawling on the court with his wheelchair on top of him. Harry calmly laid the ball in the basket.

Then he turned to wave to the crowd as it burst into cheers and applause.

Brother, Sister, and Freddy ran to Harry's side. "Way to go, Wheels!" cried Brother. "Right on!" shouted Sister and Freddy.

Too-Tall lay on the court, all tangled up in his wheelchair. The gang pried his twisted arms and legs loose from the chair and helped him to his feet. He shook the cobwebs from his head. Then he walked

toward Harry with the gang following.

"Uh-oh," said Freddy. "Here comes Too-Tall. And I'll bet he's MAD."

But to everyone's surprise, Too-Tall wasn't mad. He had been beaten so badly—so completely—that he was too shocked and amazed to be mad.

Too-Tall looked down at Harry with wide eyes. "Where'd you learn to play like that?" he asked.

"I spent three years in a wheelchair basketball league in Big Bear City," said Harry.

"Then it wasn't a fair contest," said Too-

WHERE'D YOU LEARN TO PLAY LIKE THAT?

Tall. "I only had a week to practice. If I had *three years* to practice, I'd beat you, for sure!"

"Want to set a date for three years from now?" asked Harry with a grin.

"Nah," said Too-Tall. "I ain't got time for this nonsense. Think of a game we're both already good at and you're on. For right now!"

"Hmm," said Harry. "I doubt there's anything we're both good at. The only other game I play is chess, and I'm sure you don't—"

"Chess?" said Too-Tall. "Did you say *chess*?"

Harry nodded.

"That's perfect!" cried Too-Tall.

"*You* play *chess*?" asked Harry.

"Do I play chess?" laughed Too-Tall. "Tell him, boys."

"He plays chess," said Skuzz.

"Real good," said Smirk.

"He's Champion of Bear Country School," added Vinnie.

"I can't get anybody to play me," whined Too-Tall. "I tried to teach these bums." He jabbed a thumb toward the gang. "But they stink! I joined the school chess club. But those chickens refuse to play me!"

"Then I guess chess *is* perfect," said Harry. "Last year I was Cub Champion of Big Bear City School."

Brother, Sister, and Freddy looked at one another with wide eyes. They could hardly believe what they were seeing. Not only had Harry put a stop to Too-Tall's nasty teasing, but he seemed to have made a new friend too!

Meanwhile, Too-Tall was pleading with Harry for a game of chess. "You *gotta* play me, Wheels," he whined. "You just *gotta*. I'm desperate for a decent game!"

"Glad to do it, Too-Tall," said Harry. "After all, I owe you."

Too-Tall frowned. "*You* owe *me?* For what?"

Harry smiled and said, "For giving me a great nickname."

As Harry and Too-Tall went happily off together for their first chess game, Brother and Sister and Cousin Freddy headed home. On the way, they talked about the amazing story of Harry McGill—the cub

who went from the bottom to the top of the Bear Country School popularity scale.

"But I'll tell you what's *most* amazing about all this," said Brother.

"What?" asked Freddy.

"Remember when Harry first showed up at school in his wheelchair? Who would have guessed that he would turn out to be just what we were hoping for?"

"Which was what?" asked Sister.

"A cub who can play circles around Too-Tall on the basketball court!"

Stan and Jan Berenstain began writing and illustrating books for children in the early 1960s, when their two young sons were beginning to read. That marked the start of the best-selling Berenstain Bears series. Now, with more than 95 books in print, videos, television shows, and even Berenstain Bears attractions at major amusement parks, it's hard to tell where the Bears end and the Berenstains begin!

Stan and Jan make their home in Bucks County, Pennsylvania, near their sons—Leo, a writer, and Michael, an illustrator—who are helping them with Big Chapter Books stories and pictures. They plan on writing and illustrating many more books for children, especially for their four grand-children, who keep them well in touch with the kids of today.